W9-DFX-348

THE SHOCKING TRUTH
ABOUT BOWLING SHOES

& OTHER BIZARRE TALES

Campus Life Books

After You Graduate
Against All Odds: True Stories of People
      Who Never Gave Up
Alive: Daily Devotions
Alive 2: Daily Devotions
At the Breaking Point:
      How God Helps Us Through Crisis
The Campus Life Guide to Dating
The Campus Life Guide to Making and
      Keeping Friends
The Campus Life Guide to Surviving High School
Do You Sometimes Feel Like a Nobody?
Going the Distance
Good Advice
Grow for It Journal
How to Get Good Grades
Life at McPherson High
The Life of the Party:
      A True Story of Teenage Alcoholism
The Lighter Side of Campus Life

Love, Sex & the Whole Person:
      Everything You Want to Know
A Love Story: Questions and Answers on Sex
Making Life Make Sense
Next Time I Fall in Love
Next Time I Fall in Love Journal
The New You
Peer Pressure: Making It Work for You
Personal Best: A Campus Life Guide
      to Knowing and Liking Yourself
The Shocking Truth About Bowling Shoes
      and Other Bizarre Tales
Welcome to High School
What Teenagers Are Saying about
      Drugs and Alcohol
What They Never Told Me When I Became
      a Christian
Worth the Wait: Love, Sex, and Keeping
      the Dream Alive
You Call This a Family? Making Yours Better

THE SHOCKING TRUTH
ABOUT BOWLING SHOES

& OTHER BIZARRE TALES

WILLARD A. SMARSNICK & FRIENDS

A DIVISION OF CTI
CampusLife BOOKS

ZondervanPublishingHouse
Grand Rapids, Michigan
A Division of HarperCollinsPublishers

Cover and interior design by Jeff Sharpton, PAZ Design Group
Cartoons by John McPherson

Printed in the United States of America

92 93 94 95 96 / CH / 10 9 8 7 6 5 4 3 2 1

CONTENTS

ABOUT THE YOUTHSOURCE™ PUBLISHING GROUP

YOUTHSOURCE™ books, tapes, videos, and other resources pool the expertise of three of the finest youth-ministry resource providers in the world:

Campus Life Books—publishers of the award-winning *Campus Life* magazine, for nearly fifty years helping high schoolers live Christian lives.

Youth Specialties—serving ministers to middle-school, junior-high, and high-school youth for over twenty years through books, magazines, and training events such as the National Youth Workers Convention.

Zondervan Publishing House—one of the oldest, largest, and most respected evangelical Christian publishers in the world.

Campus Life
465 Gundersen Dr.
Carol Stream, IL 60188
708/260-6200

Youth Specialties
1224 Greenfield Dr.
El Cajon, CA 92021
619/440-2333

Zondervan
5300 Patterson, S.E.
Grand Rapids, MI 49530
616/698-6900

ACKNOWLEDGMENTS

Thanks! (Really)

It wouldn't seem right to begin this list of acknowledgments without recognizing the two most important people in my life: Ralph and Betty Smarsnick. Without you, Mom and Dad, where would I be? I mean, like, really, *where would I be?* Mom, I'm obviously grateful to you for giving me an incredibly creative middle name—Alpine (a name you, of course, ripped off from your Honeymoon Hotel—The Duluth Alpine Inn). Then Dad, I'm especially grateful for your insight into both humor and photo-copy machine repair. As the promotional writeup for your first book, *Turned Loose in Duluth*, says of you: "Ralph the Zerox repairman is a one-of-a-kind original in a world of cheap copies." And, yes, Dad, may that famed father-and-son comedy team, Smarsnick & Smarsnick, ever be a bright spot in the dark corners of Duluth's night spots.

Now let's talk about my friends—as in "By Willard Alpine Smarsnick & *Friends*." A very special thanks to Jim Long, Chris Lutes and Ralph Smarsnick (my dad, again). Your deft-defying prose, off-kilter sense of humor, and oddball antics will forever live in the hearts of your five or six fans. And to show the world just how close we really are, I've decided to print only your first names after the stuff you wrote. If you have a problem with that, see my lawyer.

I would also like to thank humorist Marsha Marks for a couple of very goofy ideas; you'll find them reflected in chapter 4. Then, of course, a great big thanks to cartoonist John McPherson. Your illustrations have certainly captured something—I'm just not sure what. Seriously, I appreciate ya a bunch, funny guy.

I must mention Jim and Chris one more time (my contract says so). Without your creatively bizarre input and without your belief in me, I would still be doing standup at Lenny's Late Night Disco of Montreal. Hey, I appreciate ya.

By the way, all the stuff without a byline is by my good buddy Will B. Strange. Thanks, weirdo.

Now for all the other people I should thank ...hey, I'm out of room, OK?

Cheers!

Willard Alpine Smarsnick

DATING LIFE AT THE ZOO

& Other Scientific Studies of Animal Mayhem

ROMANCING THE AARDVARK

When I told the staff at *Campus Life* magazine that one of my life's ambitions was to do a story on the dating habits of animals, I got several looks that said something like you've got to be kidding and you've finally lost your mind.

But after engaging my fellow editors in a lively discussion about the uncanny similarities between animal and human behavior, and about how much there is to be learned of romance and love from the animal kingdom, and about how I would make their lives miserable if they didn't let me do this story, they finally gave in.

Upon receiving some encouragement, direction, and looks that said it better be good, I returned to my office (with a smile on my face), cracked my knuckles, and put my touch-tone finger to work:

pleeeep ... pleeeep ... pleeeep

"Brookfield Zoo library."

"Hello! I'm doing this really exciting story on the dating behavior of animals and I figured ..."

"Give me your number and I'll have somebody get back to you...."

Not one to wait around, and knowing a put-off when I hear it, I got back on the phone and touch-toned my way to the Houston Zoological Gardens, getting David Ruhder on the phone.

After telling me, "I'm probably not the best person to call," David went on to tell me about tree kangaroos. His comments had nothing to do with the dating habits of animals, but it was pretty interesting stuff anyway. Like, these kangaroos really do live in trees.

In time, though, he did get around to animal attraction. Lions, for instance, are actually pretty romantic creatures (if you're a lioness, that is). "Males lick the females' ears," explained David. "They show what could be called, anthropomorphically (*I love it when these guys use big words*), affection."

David then told me one of the most disturbing facts I discovered during my work on this Award-winning Piece of Biological Research: Not only do certain obnoxious human lowlifes try to attract human females by whistling, but certain types of cantaloupe do the same thing (or was that antelope?). These animals (and I do mean *animals*) will find themselves small patches of turf on the plains and start whistling at the girls. Sounds pretty sick to me.

From Houston my research took me to the nation's capital (*what better place to find zoo-y behavior?*), where I talked to Dr. Darrell Boness, a scientist at the National Zoological Park. Dr. Boness knows a lot about seals. Stuff like: *Northern fur seals grab the females with their teeth and drag them around.*

Word of caution: Guys, don't try this—you will get smacked.

"Northern fur seals," adds Dr. Boness, "show very little affectionate behavior." *No kidding.*

Realizing that I was on a roll and involved in what could only modestly be called Ground-breaking Research in the Area of Romance (*I was also having a pretty good time*), I called the Phoenix Zoo and talked to Dick George. Dick seems like a real nice guy who knows a little about scorpions (males and females arm wrestle ... or rather pincer wrestle), whooping cranes (they hop around a lot)—and garden spiders.

It seems that for the male spider to approach the female spider, he must be *very in love* and *incredibly fast on his eight little feet.*

Why? Because a female garden spider likes to have her potential mate for lunch. No, not as a guest but as the meal. This strikes me as pretty antisocial behavior. Not to mention the fact that it must be hard for a female spider to get a date.

Although I had already learned a whole lot so far, I wasn't totally satisfied with the depth of my research. There was still much to be discovered. Like, what about the love life of the armadillo?

pleeeep ... pleeeep ... pleeeep ... pleeeep
"Fort Worth Zoo."

"Hello there! I'm doing this really fascinating story on the love life of animals, and I'd like to

know something about armadillos!"

"Just a second..."

"This is Steve."

"Hi! I'm working on this incredible story on the dating and love life of animals, and I'd like to talk armadillo."

"We don't have any armadillos."

"You're in Texas and you don't have armadillos?"

"They're nasty and hard to keep."

"Oh."

Over the miles of phone line, he must have sensed the disappointment (or was that static?), because he did come up with an amazing fact: *White male rhinos can flip female rhinos into the air.* From this information I deduced an important application for female readers: *Never date white rhinos.*

Obviously I was quite distraught over my failure to glean insights into the romantic nature of armadillos. It was also disconcerting to learn that armadillos aren't the cute, cuddly critters I'd always thought they were. *Yet*, I said to myself, *there are always penguins!* (I've had a fascination for penguins ever since I saw my first tuxedo.)

pleeeep ... pleeeep ... pleeeep

"Alaska Zoo."

"Hello! I'm doing this incredible story on animal love life and I'd like to talk to an expert about penguins...."

"We don't have penguins."

"You don't have penguins?"

"No."

Obviously that fact jarred me, but an ace journalist is always quick with an alternative plan.

"Do you have birds?"

"Yes."

"May I speak with somebody who knows something about birds?"

"I'll let you speak with Tom."

pleeeep ... pleeeep

"Hello."

"Hi! I understand you guys don't have any penguins up there."

"That's right, all penguins live south of the equator. You won't find penguins living in the wild here."

"Oh."

"And since our zoo only has animals that live in Alaska, we don't have penguins."

"Oh."

Again, it was time for an alternative plan.

"Well, tell me, Tom...."

"Wayne."

"What?"

"The name's Wayne. Tom wasn't around when you called, so I took the call."

"Well then, Wayne, what can you tell me about polar bears?"

"I can tell you a lot about those; we have a lot of polar bears. Well, they're real mean and aggressive. And they travel all the time. The bulls on the move, more so than the sows."

"Wait a minute, I thought we were talking about bears, *not pigs*."

"The male polar is called a bull and the female is called a sow."

"Oh..."

Realizing it was time to move on, I thanked Tom or Wayne or whoever, and placed a call to the Bronx Zoo in New York—and there I got a chance to talk to Fred Koontz. Fred is an associate curator of mammals and knows a lot about the dating habits of hammerhead bats.

"Male hammerheads," says Fred, "will form a 'lek' in a tree—it's kind of like a singles' bar. They'll all hang from the tree and start making this noise with their voice boxes. Now keep in mind, the voice box makes up a third of the hammerhead's body length, so they can sing really loud. And what their singing sounds like is a plumber hitting a pipe with a wrench. So the female will come cruising by the tree and choose a male whose singing she really likes."

And another important point of application: *If you don't want to date a female bat, don't bang a pipe while hanging from a tree.*

As informative as Fred's story was, I still felt like I was missing something that would make this an Award-winning Article. *What this story needs,* I told myself, *is an international twist.*

pleeeep ... pleeeep ... pleeeep

"Keine something-or-other something-or-other..."

All of which said that my call to Munich (as in Germany) wasn't going through. But finally, with the persistence found only in the most seasoned of journalists (and with the help of directory assistance), I heard ...

"Münchener Tierpark Hellabrunn." Or something like that.

"Do ... you ... speak ... English?"

"Yes."

"Thank goodness. May ... I ... speak ... to ... some ... one ... who ... can ... tell ... me ... about ... animal ... dating ... habits?"

At this point there was a great deal of static (or was that laughter?), then suddenly I was talking to Peter Beyer. He's the Educational Officer at the Munich Zoo, and he also watches birds in his backyard a lot.

"Do ... you ... speak ... English?"

"Yes."

"Thank goodness. I ... am ... doing ... this ... story ... on ... animals ... and ... how ... males ... and ... females ... attract ... each ... other. Do ... you ... understand?"

"I think so. In my backyard at home I have a bird called the Birkhahn—and the male is dancing around a lot, showing off. It is like he is trying to implore [*I think he meant impress*] the female."

"That ... is ... very ... interesting.... But ... I ... was wondering ... if ... you ... have ... any ... what ... we ... would ... call ... unusual ... animals.... Like ... the ... wart ... hog."

"Would you please spell that?"

"W ... A ... R ... T ... H ... O ... G ... wart ... hog."

"I don't know the word. Let me allow you to speak to Beatrix Rau. She is a zoological assistant who might be able to help you."

pleeeep ... pleeeep

"Beatrix Rau."

"Do ... you ... speak ... English?"

"Yes."

"Thank goodness. I ... am ... doing ... this ... story ... on ... how ... male ... and ... female ... animals ... attract ... each ... other—what ... we ... call ... dating ... in ... the ... United ... States. What ... can ... you ... tell ... me ... about ... say ... wart ... hogs, or ... maybe, ... ant ... eaters?"

"That's funny, I was just thinking about

anteaters."

"What ... were ... you ... thinking?"

"I don't know. They were just in my mind, that's all."

"Do ... you ... know ... anything ... about ... the ... relationship ... between ... the ... male ... and ... female ... ant ... eater?"

"No, no, I was just thinking general things about them. I know nothing about that."

So ended my story on (and my budget for) love and romance in the animal kingdom. I can't wait to get to work on my other ideas for Award-winning Articles. Such as "Why Wombats Don't Play Football," or "Why Gila Monsters Make Poor Mascots," or how about "Clothing Hints for the naked Mole Rat"?

— *Chris*

Our highly trained investigative reporting team (actually, one guy on the phone) has uncovered through exhaustive research (actually, just a couple of phone calls) that there are *carnivorous mice* roaming around out there.

You got it, mice that eat flesh—and they also howl like wolves!

However, don't pack your bags and head for the hills just yet (even though "killer mice" do live in the Western, Southern, and Central Plains states). These monster rodents really don't munch on anything much larger than grasshoppers. Because of that nasty little habit they are commonly called "grasshopper mice" (clever name). Grasshopper mice have been known, however, to capture and devour other non-carnivorous mice (but it would probably be rather stupid to call them "mice mice").

"They love to eat grasshoppers. And they eat them like you'd eat a Popsicle," said one university researcher, who will remain unnamed because he feared we'd distort the basic facts of this story. (*Really, would we do anything like that?*)

The aforementioned unnamed source revealed that the *Onychomys leucogaster* (the creature's scientific name) will "sit back on its rear end and howl" much like the greatly feared wolf howls at the moon. Actually, says our unnamed source, the howlings of the grasshopper mouse sound more like a "teapot whistling."

So what do you expect from a rodent not much bigger than a can of tuna?

For some love-sick animals, dating truly becomes a *Huge Frustration*. Consider the blubbery tale of Humphrey, the bull elephant seal. The three-ton, fifteen-foot mammal waddled onto a dairy farm on New Zealand's northeast coast, seeking true love among a herd of cows (no, not sea cows—the four-legged kind).

In several unsuccessful attempts to woo a prospective mate, Humphrey smashed barbed wire fences and tore apart a farm gate. But the lovesick seal really became a romantic wash-out when he made amorous advances toward a 10,000-gallon water tank. The tank sprang a leak and offered him—quite fittingly—a cold shower.

A few years back the good folks of Stevens Point, Wisconsin, had this problem. You could call it *amphibian dropover*. See, these tiny frogs would come dashing (at least leaping) up this hill just outside the town's outskirts. The nearly hopped-out hoppers would then attempt to cross a four-lane highway—only to be daunted by a Major Obstacle: a road curb! *A very high road curb!* Always a leap too low, the little critters would bounce off the cement barrier and tumble helplessly into drain sewers. *But that's not the worst of it.* These drain sewers emptied into the roaring rapids of the semi-mighty Wisconsin River. Get the picture? A cold-blooded death, indeed!

Fearing that the amphibian population would *drop off* dramatically, the town's mayor, Scott Shultz, jumped forward with a plan: smooth the curb into a leap-easy access ramp. So it was done.

But, *more problems*! Once up the ramp, the tiny web-footed guys met more crushing defeat. We're talking frog road-kill here.

Enter plan #2: warning signs for motorists that feature frogs in various stages of leaping. (It should also be noted that smaller signs were erected for frogs, which showed tiny automobiles.)

But, *still more problems*! Thievery! Yes, sticky fingers kept attaching themselves to those *clever* signs. While nobody wanted to jump to hasty conclusions, there was strong speculation about the identity of said culprits. "We did find one of the signs in a dorm room over at Stevens Point's U. of Wisconsin campus," Mayor Shultz revealed to *Campus Life*'s ace reporter. So what to do?

Enter plan #3: "T-shirts!" announced the mayor. "We thought if we could offer a T-shirt featuring the leaping frog warning sign, then maybe people would leave the signs alone."

However, the mayor wasn't thoroughly convinced that a few hundred T-shirts would do the trick. More drastic measures were certainly needed. "The one sign we found—we went out there and welded it to the post," says this most-persistent mayor. "We then mounted the post in 400 pounds of concrete."

As for other measures? "Well," admits the town's chief administrator, "we don't plan to put up machine gun nests, if that's what you mean. But if the sign comes up missing again, then I guess maybe we'll need to do some more thinking."

Millions of black, fingernail-sized toads leaped their way into New Port Richey, Florida–creating massive, squiggling "carpets" on roadways and lawns.

"It looked like the whole yard was moving…. It puts me in mind of those movies, *The Bees* and *The Birds* or something," resident Donna Abshier told reporters. "We couldn't open doors because they'd hop right in."

And while toads rampaged across Florida in leaps and bounds, hundreds of peacocks terrorized ritzy La Canada Flintridge, California.

That's right—PEACOCKS! The not-so-friendly feathered friends shattered car windshields, trampled flower gardens, and broke at least one (*gasp!*) Jacuzzi canopy.

Actually the guy's name isn't Dale—it's Mark Murphy. As for the hound, it's a springer spaniel. And here's what *really happened.* Mark's mutt became trapped underwater awhile back and lapped up a little too much H_2O (which is a nice way of saying the dog's tail stopped wagging).

So Mark did what any decent, dog-loving human being would do. What *he did* was offer a little mouth-to-muzzle resuscitation. Yes, the smooched pooch eventually snapped to his feet. "It probably took about five minutes or so," Mark told reporters, "which is a long time to blow down a dog's nose."

So how have Mark's friends recognized his heroic deed? They've simply awarded him with a new nickname: "Dog breath."

KILLER TURKEY ALERT

Clutching her can of doggie Mace, mail carrier Charlotte Ingold warily approached the mailbox at John Berry's home in Cottage Hill, Illinois. But it wasn't Berry's two pit bulls that attacked the postal worker. Her dog-gone assailants turned out to be a couple of winged warriors charged forth gobbling ferociously, Charlotte instinctively raised the can of Mace and fired away. Yet the stinging spray only served to enrage the ghoulish gobblers, leading to a feathered frenzy of beak-bearing, wing-flapping mayhem. One tumultuous tom actually lunged at Charlotte's face while the other poultry-geist pecked viciously at her clothing. Before becoming gobbler cobbler, however, the beleaguered letter carrier managed to wing her way to safety. As for the two not-so-friendly feathered friends, they're being confined to Berry's turkey cage during mail delivery—keeping Charlotte protected from any further *fowl play*.

The animal liberation movement reached new slows a while back. It seems that several not-so-quick-thinking activists freed about 12,000 snails from Peter Van Poortvliet's escargot farm in eastern England. Yet the poor shelled critters simply slid from frying pan to freezer. "There's no way they can survive" outside in the cold weather, the befuddled snail farmer told reporters. So any way you look at it, those snails are escar ... *gone*.

The ruthless warrior lurks in the forest. He shows no mercy; he takes no prisoners. He's hoofed; he's dangerous. He's ... *a cute, fluffy-tailed deer?*

Captain Ian Erickson and 400 other fellow soldiers were jogging through a Florida woods, when ... ZAP! BAM! WAP! Actually the bewildered Erickson didn't know *what* hit him—until he regained consciousness a little later ... *spitting deer fur.*

Yes, the soldier of misfortune had indeed suffered a *hart attack,* leaving him with several chipped teeth, a gash in the head, and broken glasses. Captain E. had better be prepared. The next time he's out he may kick up a real fight with Bambi's fearsome friend, *Thumper.*

WHAT THEY REALLY MEAN BY "MEALS ON WHEELS"

& Other Weird Words about Curious Cuisine

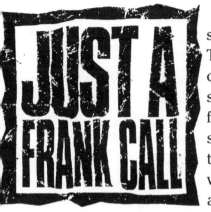

It was a balmy, slightly overcast Tuesday and the clock on the wall said 2:55. With no fast-breaking stories jumping off the *Campus Life* wire, things were as slow as maple syrup in the Arctic. I cracked my knuckles, fiddled with the stub of a No. 2 pencil, and leaned back in my worn blue chair, my boredom growing like moss on a gravestone. That's when the phone rang. I picked it up.

"Yeah," I mumbled.

"This is Andrew Rectenwal and I drive a Wienermobile."

"You do what?" I snarled, my reporter's cynicism thick as mud.

"I drive one of the six Oscar Mayer Wienermobiles now touring the country. Possibly you've seen one...."

As a matter of fact, I had. It was years ago. I was just a kid at the time, traveling cross country with the folks. We were on a four-lane highway, my old man at the wheel of our sky-blue Rambler. Then suddenly, in an oncoming lane, rolled the biggest dog on wheels I'd ever seen. I stared out the rear window until the weenie vanished from sight.

"Yes," I answered coolly, "I think maybe I've seen one." Like any seasoned reporter, I tried to remain calm and aloof. But inside I boiled with the excitement of a little kid turned loose in a cotton candy factory. "Tell me, Andrew," I asked, "how did you come to be a wiener driver? Do you do this for a living?"

"I'm a student at the University of Wisconsin. Right now I have an internship as a Wienermobile driver, and I thought your readers might like to know about the exciting opportunity of driving...."

Before he finished, though, I knew his angle, his gimmick. His grand scheme. This was not simply a friendly call. He had a product to push. He wanted a bit of free advertising for O.M. Most of all, he wanted to hook me into writing about the wiener-driving internship program. He couldn't fool me for a minute. Yet as I listened to his P.R. pitch, I couldn't stop thinking about the thrill of speeding down the highway seated in the world's largest hot dog. My next question reeked with that deep longing which invades every man's soul now and then. "So what does it take to drive a Wienermobile?"

"A clean driving record ... and you can't be a vegetarian."

I could meet both those high standards. *Just maybe* ... Then a good dose of reality slapped me in the face. Where would *Campus Life* find another ace reporter if I left to pursue a wild dream? I stuffed those visions of hot-dogging across the country into that mental file marked "So Many Uncaught Dreams." After all, I was a reporter for a major national magazine. There was no escaping it. I just had to do my job. Period. I swallowed hard and fired another question. "How would you describe the Wienermobile?"

"It's twenty-three feet long, ten feet high,

eight feet wide and weighs 5,800 pounds. It's a little like driving a Wiener-bego and handles like a Lambour-weenie...."

"Very funny," I put in wryly. "So what kind of thrill and danger goes with driving a Wienermobile?"

"Well, it was my third day on the job and I was cruising down I-90 toward Rockford, Illinois, and a cop comes roaring up, lights flashing. He pulls me over, looks me squarely in the eye and says, "You haven't done anything wrong. I just have to have my picture taken beside the Wienermobile.""

I knew how the man in Smokebrown felt. It would be a temptation no one could resist. Imagine capturing that cherished memory on a 5x7 glossy. *Just you and you alone, leaning against the Wienermobile*. Again, I fought back the strong emotions that could drive a guy crazy. It was time, if only for my own sanity, to call this case closed. I asked what I intended to be my final question. "When will you be driving the Wienermobile again?"

"My partner and I are driving right now. Actually, my partner is driving and I'm talking to you on the cellular phone...."

Cellular phone ... *the weeniemobile has a cellular phone*. All the luxuries of life, inside one freewheeling frankfurter...

Once again my misguided muse drove me back to those childhood memories. Then suddenly Andrew's slick-as-slime spiel jerked me back to the conversation. "Would you like to ride in the Wienermobile sometime?"

"Really?" The excitement oozed from my voice like jelly in a filled donut.

"We're in Reno right now, but in a few weeks we'll be in Chicago. We'll be glad to drop by and give you a ride."

As I put down the receiver that day, I realized the offer was probably just so much P.R. shmooze. Maybe I'd never hear from this Andrew Rectenwal again. Maybe that kid-sized view from the Rambler would be as close as I'd ever get to my dream. Yet I couldn't get the image out of my head. Me, flying down the road without a care in the world, in a Wienermobile. I knew my life would never be the same after that phone call.

— *Ralph*

A few years ago, Dr. E. Lendell Cockrum, professor of ecological studies at the University of Arizona, stood before his students and led a fairly innocuous discussion on "protein sources." And while it was pretty much a subpoint, Dr. Cockrum recalls mentioning "certain types of rats" in his lecture. After all, he later told *Campus Life* magazine, "pack rats *did* serve as food for American Indians."

Anyway, as a result of the prof's passing comments, a few students decided to expand their diet to include, as Dr. Cockrum puts it, "the genus Rattus." And out of it all developed an Arizona U.-based organization called SONE: Secret Order of *Neotoma* Eaters. (If you didn't guess, *Neotoma* is the biological name for *pack rat.*)

Don't get SONE wrong, though. They're not some weird, wacko group or anything (*well, not too weird and wacko*). They *don't eat* sewer rats, which are well-known disease carriers. They're strictly into the healthy, field rat variety. And the rats *are* carefully prepared— charcoal grilled through and through. *And smeared with a lot of barbecue sauce.*

Of course, you're wondering: *What does a cooked rat taste like?* "The feelings on that are mixed," says Elaine Johnson, a lifetime member of SONE. "Some say chicken, some say ham. Others think it tastes a lot like the barbecue sauce."

IF THEY SQUIGGLE THEY'RE NOT DONE

Here, according to naturalist Dan Belting, is a recipe to tickle (or cripple) the taste buds:

(1) Get a dozen two-inch-long "real skinny" angle-worms. (Don't use night crawlers, they're too tough.)

(2) Blanch the squiggly guys to death in a pot of boiling water.

(3) Take out of boiling water. Dice 'em into several pieces, then toss them into a clean pot of boiling water. This step helps remove the non-digestible dirt.

(4) Remove and boil them one more time to

remove any excess soil.

(5) Stir them up in your favorite cookie batter and serve.

... And you only *thought* those light-colored things in Mom's secret cookie recipe were butterscotch chips.

EAT UP EVERYONE! THERE'S PLENTY MORE WORM PIE WHERE THIS CAME FROM!

JUST A PAIR OF ODOR EATERS

Warning: Improving your health may be hazardous to your breath. Just ask Tomi Ilves and Paul Martikainen of Lake Worth, Florida. It seems the two health-conscious pals had heard somewhere that garlic cleanses the blood and lowers blood pressure. And let's just say they wanted *really* clean blood and *really low* blood pressure. So one Thursday morning a while back, they started the school day off by eating garlic. Between them they consumed around eight entire bulbs of the smelly stuff. Needless to say, their garlic munching raised a real stink at Lake Worth

High. After being told more than once to stop gobbling garlic, the guys were finally ushered out the door by the principal. In fact, their odious behavior earned them three days of suspension. Of course, T&P can't quite figure out why everybody got so sniffy over the whole odoriferous affair. "This wasn't like we were doing it on purpose to get anybody mad," Paul told one reporter. "We were blowing in each other's face and we couldn't sense a garlic smell."

What can we say, guys, but ... *that really stinks.*

If Tabby coughs up a clump of hair, it's no cause for alarm. Fur balls form internally as a part of normal feline grooming. But ingested hair can be rather, well, *hairy* for humans— *especially longer-haired humans who chew nervously on the end of their locks.* Case in point: Surgeons at Alavi Hospital in Shiraz, Iran, actually removed a 4.4-pound solid ball of hair from a 21-year-old woman. "Unlike cats," reported *Omni* magazine, "who usually vomit or cough up the excess hair they swallow, humans are faced with more serious consequences." *Fur sure ... fur sure ...*

A LITTLE JUST DESSERTS

For two robbers who walked into a pastry shop in St. Etienne, France, it probably looked like an easy rip-off. But when they demanded the goods, armed with a pistol and a tear-gas bomb, they were met instead with a barrage of the goodies.

The sixty-five-year-old pastry shop owner, along with her daughter and two grandchildren, thwarted the would-be thieves with a pastry pummeling of cream-filled pies and cakes. No match for the sweet attack, the robbers fled the scene of the cream.

A REAL TASTE FOR ART

Poor Myrtle Young. There she was, over at a big convention in Fort Wayne, Indiana, and guess what happened? This local yokel sauntered over and chewed up her prized sand dollar. Well, it wasn't really a sand dollar. You see, Myrtle used to work as a potato chip inspector for Seyfert's Foods. And it seems that one day her watchful eye started seeing things: faces of famous people, animals ... and at least one sand dollar. So Myrtle started collecting these unusual chip shapes. As a result, it didn't take long for the old chip checker to become somewhat famous. She and her collection have even appeared on Letterman and Carson. She's also shown her works of potato art at various conventions around the nation—which brings us back to *Fort Wayne*.

Here's how Myrtle described the grizzly (uh, that's *greasy*) potato crime: "There were quite a few people standing around, and I was telling them about my chip collection. This one man reached through [the crowd] quickly and took one."

Of course, the would-be crumbler of Myrtle's dreams was quickly nabbed and forced to cough up the evidence—something he didn't mind doing. The chip *was* pretty stale, admitted the not-so-chipper chip snatcher.

THE OFFICIAL CAMPUS LIFE HEALTH-FREE DIET

We're sick and tired of all the bad press junk food is getting these days. You know it; we know it: Ding Dongs and Twix bars are good for you! We've done the research to prove it. It's all there on the wrappers—the Recommended Daily Allowance (R.D.A.) of protein, vitamins, and iron the government says you need to be healthy! So, with a box of Twinkies held high, our Junk Food Research Team proudly presents the The Official *Campus Life* Magazine Health-Free Diet.

Simply pick one junk food item from each of the groups below, eat the quantities suggested, and you will be assured all the vitamins and nutrients you need each day!

Protein
 25 Twinkies
 50 Twix
 16.66 Butterfingers
 25 Pop Tarts
 5 boxes of Doo Dads
 25 regular-size orders of McDonalds
    french fries
or 9.09 gallons of Cambell's
    Cream of Asparagus Soup

Vitamin A

> 50 Three Musketeers Ice Cream Bars
> 4 gallons of Spaghetti-Os
> 12.5 Ding Dongs
> 10 Pop Tarts
> or 4.5 gallons of Campbell's
>   Cream of Asparagus Soup

Vitamin C

> 103 pieces of Skittles candy
> 5 gallons of Kool-Aid
> 50 McDonald's Big Macs
> 5 McDonald's apple pies
> or 9.09 gallons of Campbell's
>   Cream of Asparagus Soup

Thiamine

> 6.66 bags of Ruffles potato chips
> 12.5 Ding Dongs
> 12.5 McDonald's chocolate shakes
> 10 Pop Tarts
> or 9.09 gallons of Campbell's
>   Cream of Asparagus Soup

Riboflavin

> 50 Twix
> 25 Butterfingers
> 25 Twinkies
> 10 Pop Tarts
> or 9.09 gallons of Campbell's
>   Cream of Asparagus Soup

EAT UP. YOU NEED TO HAVE 37 MORE SNICKERS BARS TO FULFILL YOUR DAILY REQUIREMENT OF PROTEIN.

Niacin

100 McDonald's Chicken McNuggets
(Add 25 packets of McDonald's
Barbeque Sauce and you'll get your
Recommended Daily Allowance of
vitamins C and A.)
50 McDonald's chocolate shakes
5.5 bags of Chee-tos
10 Pop Tarts
or 9.09 gallons of Campbell's
Cream of Asparagus Soup

Calcium

9.09 gallons of Spaghetti-Os
50 Butterfingers
25 Three Musketeers Ice Cream Bars
50 Ding Dongs
or 9.09 gallons of Campbell's
Cream of Asparagus Soup

Iron

50 Kit Kats
25 Butterfingers
10 Pop Tarts
or 9.09 gallons of Campbell's
Cream of Asparagus Soup

Vitamin D

50 Kit Kats
10 Pop Tarts
Soup won't help.

Vitamin B6

10 Pop Tarts
About a half a pound of Ruffles potato
chips
Sadly, soup won't help.

Phosphorus

    25 Pop Tarts
    5.5 bags of Chee-tos
    16.66 Pudding Pops
    Tragically, soup will not provide this.

Magnesium

    50 Pop Tarts
    .75 bags of Ruffles potato chips
    16.66 Butterfingers
    50 Pudding Pops
    No soup, friends.

Zinc

    50 Pop Tarts
    7 bowls of Ghostbusters cereal
    Need we say it?

Copper

    25 Pop Tarts
    No soup.

Highly Recommended Simplified Diets

The following diets allow you to concentrate exclusively on one food source, and are, therefore, quite convenient.

Asparagus Soup Delight Diet

This diet is especially recommended for soup lovers and for avid can recyclers. However, you will forfeit your Recommended Daily Allowance of vitamins D and B6, as well as phosphorus, magnesium, zinc, and copper; so, as you can see, there are trade-offs.

Breakfast

    2 gallons of Campbell's Cream of Asparagus
    Soup

Lunch
2 gallons of Campbell's Cream of Asparagus Soup

Dinner
5 gallons of Campbell's Cream of Asparagus Soup

Midnight Snack
.09 gallons of Campbell's Cream of Asparagus Soup

Some diligent dieters have found it helpful to simply fill their bathtub with Campbell's Cream of Asparagus Soup once a day. Ten gallons works nicely. The .91 gallons that you do not eat can be used, with Drano, to flush out the drain.

Caloric Intake Information. Please realize this is not a *reducing* diet. The Asparagus Soup Delight Diet will net you 13,090 calories a day. If you exercise moderately and you're a 150-pound male, you'd gain about twenty pounds after a week on this diet. If you're a female, you'd gain about twenty-two pounds. We said there were trade-offs.

Pop Tart Diet
If pantry space is at a premium, or if you are traveling, or if you do not have a bathtub, we would suggest you consider the popular Pop Tart Diet.

Breakfast
5 Pop Tarts

Lunch

    2 Pop Tarts

Dinner

    3 Pop Tarts

Five Pop Tarts will give your morning some lift, and you will quickly come to appreciate the lighter lunch and dinner menus. Unfortunately, the Pop Tart Diet does not provide your vitamin C, though 103 Skittles candies will correct that deficiency. Your neglected calcium can be derived from 12.5 Pudding Pops, a fine dinner-time dessert. It should also be noted that this diet will only provide one-fifth of your Recommended Daily Allowance of zinc and magnesium, and slightly less than half of your protein, phosphorus, and copper. It is, therefore, advisable to alternate weeks with the Pop Tart Diet and the Asparagus Soup Delight Diet.

Caloric Intake Information. This whole diet, complete with Skittles and Pudding Pops, will give you only 3,440 calories a day. A male Pop Tart dieter might only gain half a pound or so a week; a female, two to three pounds. Add a few extra miles to your morning workout, and this is a wonderful maintenance diet.

Ding Dong Diet

Finally, we've had many requests for help in constructing a sound Ding Dong Diet. This is tricky, as you can imagine, because the RDDDL (Recommended Daily Ding Dong Level) varies from one nutrient to the next. The following diet has been shown to represent a reasonable compromise, provided it is not relied on solely.

Breakfast

    20 Ding Dongs

Lunch

    15 Ding Dongs

Dinner

    15 Ding Dongs

Along with exceeding the Recommended Daily Allowance (and the RDDDL) for certain nutrients, the Ding Dong Diet is also calcium rich—offering 100 percent of your R.D.A. of that essential dietary ingredient. The missing vitamin C can be supplied simply by drinking 5 gallons of Kool-Aid with either lunch or dinner (your choice). Unfortunately, this diet leaves you without your vitamin D or B6, and minus those essential minerals the U.S.D.A. suggests. We, therefore, urge you: Whenever possible, order the soup.

Caloric Intake Information.
Total calories per day: 8,500 (more, of course, if you add the Kool-Aid). A male will gain about eleven pounds a week; a female, twelve to thirteen pounds. So what's a few extra pounds, here and there?

                                                   — Jim

3

ATTACK OF THE ACCORDION TERRORISTS

& Other Reasons to Invest in Earplugs

ACCORDION

TERRORISTS BELLOW AWAY FOR THEIR

RIGHT TO BE HEARD

It all began one evening in June when several crazed terrorists strode briskly into a San Francisco restaurant. With their faces concealed by triangular bandannas and dark glasses, they positioned themselves strategically in the middle of the crowd of dazed diners. All armed with the same instrument of destruction, the black-leather-jacketed band commenced their merciless attack on unsuspecting patrons and restaurant workers.

"What we did," conspirator Tom Torriglia told *Campus Life* magazine in an exclusive interview, "was play the 'Beer Barrel Polka' and 'Lady of Spain' on our accordions—at least we played until they kicked us out."

But that restaurant raid wasn't the only ear assault these squeeze-box guerrillas committed on that June evening. During their hours of accordion terror, the self-proclaimed "accordionistas" (also known as the Accordion Liberation Front) stormed thirty-six different San Francisco night spots.

In retrospect, it must be asked: Why this brutal aural assault?

"June is National Accordion Awareness Month," said the matter-of-fact Torriglia. "We wanted to bring attention to that important time of the year."

Of course, accordion awareness represents

only a small part of the ongoing battle these squeeze-box freedom fighters are currently waging. Their goal (a terrifying one indeed) is to alter the very nature of society. Specifically, they want to make the accordion a respectable instrument.

Even fanatical accordionistas, however, are somewhat in tune with reality. Change, they readily admitted, doesn't occur after a one-night accordion siege. "What we are trying to do now," said Big Lou, founder of the Accordion Liberation Front, "is get the accordion named the official instrument of San Francisco—then we'll go from there."

"Going from there" also means forming a for-real (if that's possible) accordion band. Calling themselves "Those Darn Accordions!" (for obvious reasons), Big Lou, Torriglia, and the rest continue to bring their own brand of musical horror to the Bay area.

"What kind of music do we offer?" Torriglia asked rhetorically. "We play your standard accordion tunes, but we also play the theme from the old *Perry Mason* show. And we play 'Satisfaction' by the Stones."

Yet anyone who thinks Those Darn Accordions! can *really* crank out rock and roll, must think again.

"It all kind of sounds like a polka," confessed Torriglia.

— Chris

Significant things are happening in the underground, alternative music movement. Many of these new-music groups have little to say that's worth hearing. Occasion-ally, however, you encounter a band that is simultaneously innovative and thought-provok-ing. Ohio's own Screaming Swill & Rachel is such a group. Backed by The Gophers, SS&R have created a rock classic with their latest release, Claustrophobic Mole, *on the UnderDog label. It is currently enjoying good college radio play in certain areas of the country (principally in the Cleveland suburbs).* Campus Life *recently interviewed the young husband-wife team in Cleveland, where the family had gathered for their annual winter picnic at the zoo. What follows is a condensation of that interview.*

Campus Life: I'd like to start off with the one question I've always wanted to ask you guys: Why is it that year after year you two just keep using the same publicity photo?

Screaming Swill: Well, it's kind of sym-bolic.

Rachel: We just really like the photo for one thing. We're from Cleveland, sorry to say, but this suburban Chicago photographer did the photo back when we were still going together, before we got married, and we think it turned out great. We even used it as our wedding picture (which is our only conces-sion to being mushy and romantic). Then we thought, *What a trip! This could be the ultimate P.R. gimmick. We could be the first band ever to use the same P.R. photo for their entire career!* You might say that the possibility captured our imagination.

SS: All that's true, but there was also some deep symbolism to it. We figured we looked so young and fresh in that photo, and that parallels what we want to do with our music. We want it to be ever young and fresh. I mean, look at the photos of the Stones and The Who. Do they look young and fresh? Course not. I rest my case.

CL: So that was the inside joke behind your new song, "Frozen in Time"?

R: Right.

> *Like aging rockers*
> > *Hiding there behind a photo of*

them young
We're frozen
Frozen in time

SS: And then these lines give it the Swill & Rachel twist:

> *But don't ever think*
> > *That all of this is just a silly whim*
> > *No, it's well thought-out*
> > *We're all thawed out*
> > *Though frozen*
> > *Frozen in time*

CL: I know artists are always a bit reluctant to explain their work, but could you fill us in a bit on the concept behind your new album, *Claustrophobic Mole?* It earned you accolades from leading underground publications.

SS: Yo. Being recognized by our peers is

heavy. It's kind of humbling, ya know? Makes me wanna scream.

R: Everything makes you wanna scream.

SS: Oh yeah, sure, sure, fine, OK, Rach.

R: Swill and I, like, we were at the public library reading back issues of *Garden Science* magazine—just something we do on slow Saturdays—and, I don't know, something captured Swill's imagination.

SS: Yeah, well, there was this photo feature on moles. And they just looked so squeezed and squashed in their little tunnels. And they liked living in the dark and dirt. I mean, it's like those creatures eat dirt!

R: When Swill saw that, it was like his mind was blown by this heavy-duty concept. And man, when that happens, it's best just to stay out of the way and give the man air, 'cause you just know there's going to be this cosmic creative explosion.

SS: It was like that, too. I said to myself: *Mole, tunnel, dirt, dinner.* Kept saying that over and over again. It had a ring to it. I knew right then it was going to be part of a major lyric thing. An awesome metaphor was materializing before the eyes of my brain, you know?

R: Pretty soon, right there in the public library, Swill is mouthing these song lyrics. At first he was just saying them to himself. Before long he's, like, saying them right out loud. Not quite screaming, but louder than he ought to be in a library. I mean, Swill and I are law-abiding citizens, not rebellious punk-types.

SS: Besides, as Rachel reminded me right then, the librarian has often stolen some of our best ideas. I'm sitting there in the periodical section and the resource librarian is listening to my creative explosions, writing down what I sing, then faxing it to Weird Al, Steve Taylor, whoever.

CL: That's quite an accusation. But tell me, what were these lyrics you were singing, what did they mean, and how did they fit in with the final album concept?

SS: OK, OK. Here's how it worked out. I wrote the words on the blank space of the mole article I was reading in *Garden Science*.

R: Then he had to pay for the magazine. What a trip! [*Laughter.*]

SS: Easy, Rach. OK, the chorus, you know, it went like this:

> *Mole, tunnel, dirt, dinner*
> *Furry critter, slimy sinner*
> *You're living in a deep, dark, fantasy*
> *   world.*

Are you a claustrophobic mole?
Or what?

See the analogy, man? Like we eat dirt, too. And we don't like the light. Dig us up into the daylight and we fight and squirm like the cruddy little moles that we are. But as long as we stay underground, hiding from the real world, we're just gonna be trapped in tunnels of darkness that go nowhere.

R: But it's really beautiful, Swill, the way you took that idea and turned it around. Tell 'em 'bout that.

SS: Yeah, well, see, some of us moles don't mind. Dirt's home, man. But there are these other moles that just get this yearning for the real world. They are the claustrophobic moles, the ones who know something's not quite right. They feel all squished up in their soiled life, and they're tired of dirt dinners. They're ready to risk everything they know in order to find some new life. That inspired the song's bridge:

Hey! Say!
Claustrophobic mole
Can you face the light?
Let it blaze and burn
Till it incinerates your night sight
Don't sweat it, man
New eyes are comin' to you!

CL: I understand you even utilized some unusual special effects on the final recording.

SS: Sure enough. Rachel and I shared the vocals. And she attacked her drums like the maniac she is. Whew! Power drumming. I handled the guitars and the Skil saw. Now, you know us, we are a guitar and Skil-saw band. We're not into keyboards. I mean, I practically live in my "Synthesizers Are for Sissies" T-shirt. But we did sell our dog to buy a Roland S-750 sampler, then we sampled actual mole sounds—had to push my Audio-Technica microphone down a mole hole with a plumber's snake. But it was worth it. Then Rach triggered the samples from her Octapad. Eerie!

CL: Rachel, you guys have a new backup band, The Gophers, and an amazing new release on the UnderDog label. What's ahead for Screaming Swill & Rachel? Will *Claustrophobic Mole* finally break you into the mainstream?

R: No way. We're destined to be an underground band, with a small but loyal following.

Besides, if we get too successful we might have to do new P.R. photos, and that would be the ultimate artistic compromise.

— *Jim*

Imagine this: a Roving Rover Musical Alarm Watch. It jumps on your bed and wakes you with an opening drum solo, follows you to the bathroom with a guitar riff, and finishes your morning wake-up tune with a slick synth crescendo in the kitchen.

Well, the Waters family of Shrewsbury, England, may have just tuned the world into this one. Here's how it happened.

At exactly 6:45, for two mornings in a row, Betty Waters thought she heard strains of the big band song, "American Patrol." But when she attempted to locate the source of the tune, she couldn't believe her ears: the Waters' family dog, Fudge. An X-ray examination by a local vet confirmed that the pooch had gulped down a musical alarm watch, which had been programmed to play the classic Glenn Miller arrangement.

If puttin' in the hits catches on (it certainly would add new meaning to the term *woofer*), maybe dog-food makers will start packing a musical alarm clock inside each can of food. Possible ingredients: horse meat, salt and *featured artist:*... Pet Shop Boys ... Toto ... Prince.

You read right—*that's trash, not thrash.* And the music is created by a group with the straightforward name of Music for Homemade Instruments. All trained musicians, MHI actually creates tunes that sound more classical than anything else—with a bit of reggae and rap tossed in here and there. But make no mistake—they do play *trash.* "We use strips of metal, racks from old refrigerators, cardboard tubes, coffee cans, whatever you have around the house or can find in a trash dumpster," band member Carole Weber told *Campus Life*

magazine. "We've even made music by plunking the spokes of bicycle tires. And in our last concert, we took this large tube and bounced it, end over end, across the stage—*made a great sound!*"

Catch'em soon at a ... *dump near you.*

SHOWER CURTAIN CALL FOR **MUSIC BUFFS**

Male vocalists in England received an entertaining offer a while back: You may audition for the Timsbury Male Choir *in the privacy of your own bathroom.*

Tired of watching a lot of raw talent go down the drain, officials of the all-male choir, located near Bath (*no kidding*), England, wanted to whet the appetites of Britain's shier bathtub baritones. Ken Sanderson, the "brains" behind the idea, says: "Many men with great voices would be a worthy asset to the choir, but they are too scared to stand up and sing in public.

So we plan to visit interested parties in the comfort of their homes. We will simply stand outside the bathroom while they get on with it."

If Sanderson's idea isn't a washout, you can expect shower curtains to rise on stages around the world, with choirs belting out their well-scrubbed tunes to soaped-out audiences. *Encore! Encore!* And pass the shampoo, please....

Yngwie Malmsteen, duck out of the way! Those wild and crazy Spinosa brothers are putting some *real muscle* into ax-handling these days. Now, we're not talking slick riffs here. What Tim and bro Travis are really into is *guitar tossing*. That's right, *these guys throw guitars.*

And, as far as we know, Tim holds the world record for pitching the metal ax a grand total of eighty-nine feet. Travis, who's apparently more into light rock, holds the acoustic toss record of fifty-six feet.

Mimicking the style of Olympic hammer throwers, the Spinosas may or may not be able to launch a career hurling guitars. Yet for the moment, we'll simply say they're a *smashing success*.

It sounds like a cagey ploy to market Bach in the barnyard. Yet an Israeli scientist claims that classical music does indeed soothe the savage chicken breast. And a calmer, happier hen, says the fowl scientist, makes a plumper, juicier bird on the table.

If farmers do decide to pipe in highbrow for their brooding-house beauties, they could be in for a surprise. Cultured poultry may stop acting like birdbrains and suddenly turn into ... real eggheads.

BETTER MEOW OR ELSE

Musical felines received the "thrill" of their nine lives a while back when Ralston Purina held a nationwide singing cat search. The grand prize for the most melodious mouser was $25,000 and a leading part in a Meow Mix cat food commercial. The big evening, which took place at New York's Lincoln Center, featured a forty-piece orchestra to accompany the four-footed stars.

To handle the quirky silence of fastidious felines, Purina decided to record the catcalls, then have the animals "lip sync" during the live performance.

Still, there was the problem of getting kitty to meow in the first place (oh, the trials of potential stardom). So during recording sessions, Purina devised this four-step plan:

(1) charm with Meow Mix;

(2) cajole with tuna;

(3) coerce by locking the animal in a closet;

(4) if the cat hadn't worked up a melody by this point, throw the tightlipped tabby in the slammer! Well, at least in a travel box.

Some cat lovers were appalled by the procedure—especially since all of the steps weren't always followed. One cat who refused to respond to Meow Mix was immediately tossed in the travel box. And, said Patti Goldstein, who was in charge of the recording session, "Going in the travel box makes them think they're headed for the veterinarian." Thus turning a mute mouser into a screeching soprano.

A not-at-all-impressed Ward Howland (Get it? HOWLand), of the Anti-Cruelty Society, said, "This is a moral issue. It's totally degrading to animals."

But Joe Raposo, who composed the music the cats caterwauled to, said *tout au contraire!* Raposo had his stringed instrument players put away their catgut for steel and nylon—at least for the Meow Off event. "It's a sensitive thing," he said.

BOGUS BAND 2: THE REVIEW

Energy Equals by MC Square on the Bogus Toonz label.

In what *Billbored* magazine has heralded the music industry's greatest surprise of the year, three guys with Bozo haircuts rap mathematical equations and scientific trivia against a backdrop of angular accompaniment. Though the first single, "Scientific American," is shallow and excessively patriotic, these rappers prove the theory of their worth and staying power on more than half of the record's ten cuts. "2 Good 2 Be 4 Gotten" eulogizes Clarence Darrow and belies the band's Fundamentalist sympathies. Actual, digitally enhanced, rare recordings of Darrow's courtroom soliloquies intercut the droning ramble of Darwinian theory. "Relativity" draws an elaborate parallel between the alienation of disintegrating family structures and Einstein's celebrated theory, while "UB Green" delineates the threat of global warming. On both "Radiation 4 U" and "Fission Fusion," MC Square delivers timely warning of the peril of scientific discoveries falling into the wrong hands. Three songs later (obviously a purposeful sequence), the recording climaxes with the back-to-back hits "Stellar Collapse" and "Theory Big Bang." The swirling galactic rhythms of the first give way to the ever-expanding instrumentation of the second, until the swelling volume is suddenly swallowed up in eight seconds of discordant chaos. The album ends with the sound of steam escaping from a broken radiator—another actual digital recording, captured on location on the shoulder of L.A.'s Santa Monica freeway. Such creative touches set MC Square apart from rap's rank and file, while proving the rap genre capable of taking us to conceptual worlds yet to be explored. On the strength of such creative impulse alone, *Energy Equals* by MC Square deserves our highest rating: five mushrooms.

— Jim

THE GREAT LOCKER HOAX

& Other "True Stories" for the Gullible

LOCKERS ARE HAZARDOUS TO YOUR HEALTH?

WASHINGTON, D.C. — They traveled from high schools across the nation. Their hometowns included Buffalo, Wyoming; Odessa, Texas; Skowhegan, Maine; Floyd, Kentucky; and Wabaunsee, Kansas. Almost all of them wore black T-shirts proclaiming **SAVE THIS ENDANGERED SPECIES!** Silk screened under the bold, silver lettering was the object of their concern: a standard-sized, unassuming locker.

The small but committed group of students assembled recently on the steps of the nation's capitol to protest the controversial "Anti-Locker Safety Act." This newly passed legislation will outlaw lockers on all high-school campuses within the next few months. So far the law is being enforced in several schools around the country. Alaska remains the only state "actively opposed" to the anti-locker ruling. During a bipartisan House committee meeting, Congresswoman Sylvia E. Soom (R-AK) stated: "No way will Alaska enforce [such a ruling]! No Way! The bill is just plain absurd!"

Many other legislators, however, disagree with Soom's assessment. "I believe wholeheartedly in the removal of lockers from public schools, " says Senator Leonard Rotag (D-FL). "Let me assure you, I voted for this bill because I care about the health and well-being of our nation's young people."

Anti-locker proponents claim that lockers are hazardous and cite dozens of cases where the metal storage units have been jerked from the wall, often landing on unsuspecting students and teachers. In a few instances, serious injuries have been reported.

"There's also the phenomenon known as 'locker incarceration,'" says Marvin Rotinaj, chief officer for the government's High School Custodial Service Department. (HSCSD is a branch of the Department of Health and Human Services.)

"Locker incarceration occurs," explains Rotinaj, "when students are accidentally *or intentionally* imprisoned inside a locker for extended periods of time.... Believe me, our research proves that it happens in schools across America *every single day.*"

Other reasons supporters cite for anti-locker legislation:

Lockers are unattractive. "They detract from the overall aesthetic appeal of our schools' hallways," claims head custodian Rotinaj.

"Lockers are simply ugly."

Lockers are unhealthy and unsanitary. Advocates of the new law argue that partially eaten lunches stored in lockers attract harmful, disease-spreading mold, insects, and rodents. Further, gym clothes (especially socks) left in lockers over extended periods of time are said to create harmful odors.

Lockers are impractical. "What real function do they serve?" asks Senator Lance Reisooh (R-IN). "Lockers constantly jam and they take up too much space in already overcrowded hallways. They're simply in the way."

Of course, many students are outraged at the ban and contend their rights are being violated. "Arguments for banning lockers are so lame, I can't believe it's gone this far," says Mark Yobwoc from Wyoming's Buffalo Community High School. (BCH is scheduled for full-scale locker removal within the next few weeks.)

Yobwoc, organizer of the recent pro-locker rally in Washington and founder of Students Together Against Locker Loathers (STALL), told *Campus Life* magazine: "I actually learned about the legislation by accident. I was working on a civics report in the library when I came across this stuff about the government wanting to remove lockers.

What next? Desks? Pencils? Gym shorts? ...

"The whole thing is just plain nuts. Students

must band together and put a stop to this nonsense— *now!*"

"It's not that easy," remarks Legislator Daffney Selegnasol (R-CA). "It's a most complex issue. We must give the bill a chance to work, then in a year we'll re-evaluate."

In the meantime, growing numbers of students face a very practical problem. "So where are we supposed to put our stuff?" complains Nan Odanrot of Wabaunsee Senior High. "Has anybody thought of that?"

Shortly after printing its startling report on lockers, Campus Life magazine started hearing from students, teachers, principals, superintendents, parents, and congressional offices. Here are excerpts from several letters (names have been dropped to protect the gullibly impaired):

I am shocked that the government would ban the use of lockers in high schools across the states.

—*Ohio*

Where *are* we supposed to put our stuff anyway? My whole science class hated the idea of taking them out.

—*Arizona*

Hats off to Silvia E. Soom of Alaska! At least someone in the legislature has brains.

—*South Carolina*

You would think the state legislators would have better things to do than consider locker legislation.

—*New Jersey*

In the article, "Lockers are Hazardous to Your Health?" it would be good to know the legislative number of the Anti-Locker Safety Act Bill, so people could look it up in the *Congressional Record* and find out which Senators and Representatives supported this act.

—*Nebraska*

Several schools have contacted our office as to whether there is any truth in the article's contention that our Congress has passed a law requiring the removal of lockers within the confines of our schools.

As Director of School Surveys and Planning for the State, I am very interested in where the information for this article originated.

—*Nebraska Department of Education*

And those were just a few letters. There were many more. One school district, deep in the middle of budget planning, wrote to ask if they should not budget money for lockers in their new school. Then there was the reporter who called, saying he'd looked through a few years of the Congressional Record. *And would you believe it? He couldn't find the name of any of the legislators quoted. Eventually,* Campus Life *magazine did let everybody in on its little joke—stating that the article was "totally bogus. A spoof. You know, satire. Something we did for your amusement. No harm, or truth meant. To be perfectly clear: YOUR LOCKER WILL NOT BE REMOVED ... So relax." We also (eventually) revealed the seven clues in the article that put a backwards spin on the spoof. (Check out the last names of each person quoted; read them backwards.)*

That should have been the end of what became known as the Great Locker Hoax, right? Wrong. More phone calls. More letters ...

Many hours of research have been conducted regarding the authenticity of this article as well as consultation with attorneys.... The least the reporter could have done is sign the article "Mickey Mouse" on assignment.
    —*School Superintendent, Nebraska*

I'd like to take exception with the approach your magazine took with the "Great Locker Hoax" article.... I made calls to our state's Principals' Association and Department of Education legal counsel seeking verification of the article.... Humor has its place but not at the expense of individuals and public institutions in this case....
    —*School Principal, Nebraska*

As a former school board member, I took your story to be the *truth* and did the following:

(1) Notified [the] school superintendent and the school board chairpersons. (The [local] superintendent asked the Minnesota Education Department about this controversial "Anti-locker Safety Law.")

(2) Made copies [of the article] for both above parties and the Minnesota School Board Association, asking them to find out if this was a law.

(3) [Contacted] the Minnesota School Board Association to learn more information.

(4) Called my local U.S. Senator's office to check out the "Anti-locker Safety Law."

There is no question that other readers went to uncalled-for expense to check out your article that they took for truth! ...

—*Minnesota*

... And one more letter:

I think it would be a good idea to exile Christopher Lutes to Bangor, Maine, for creating such a flap over the removal of lockers from our schools. Thank you for listening to my opinion in this matter.

—*Indiana*

And that last one was written by my own mother. No kidding. Sometimes life is just a little too strange to be believed.

—*Chris*

HIGHER PANTS BRING LONG LIFE!

Exclusive! The Secret to Longevity Revealed!

"It's All in the Jeans!" says Professor from Honolulu U. In an exclusive interview with the *Campus Enquirer*, Horace Boisnester, Doctor of Aging (DOA) and five-time recipient of the "Ponce de Leon Search for Eternal Youth Award," offered startling insights into longevity *and clothing style*.

"Well, let us begin with the male species. I'm positive long life has much to do with the way one wears the pants," reveals Dr. Boisnester.

After studying 1,407 octogenarians, the expert in cryogenics and polyester fashion discovered that "the older someone looks, the higher he hikes his pants...until at a great age, the belt buckle nicks the underside of the chin. This obviously endows him with the gift of long life!

"So you want to live long?" concludes Dr. Boisnester. "Well, if you're a man, pull your pants up real high ... like right under the armpits!

"As for women ... the evidence is far less conclusive, but

extended life appears to have something to do with the rolling of nylon stockings."

—*Marsha*

Exclusive! The Untold Fast-food Threat

Dr. Leola Frakleman, author of *UFOs Ate My Dog* and home-ec teacher at Butte (MT) High, has just released a conclusive report on the long-term effects of fast-food eating and employment. Doing undercover work on weekends flipping burgers at Wendy's (and making a few extra bucks on the side), Frakleman has done hundreds of case studies on fast-food junkies. Her conclusions:

Fast food creates drastic shifts in hairstyles. "Take Marsha," says Frakleman, "she has totally integrated her job at the Taco Shed into her personal grooming. Throughout the week, she can be seen wearing either her Twin Taco Do or, her personal favorite, the Frizzed Nacho Grande ... with guacamole mousse on the side."

Employment at fast-food restaurants causes severe mental confusion. "Because of his part-time job at Burger Haven," reports scientist Frakleman, "Frank can't avoid answering all questions as if they came over a drive-thru intercom. This obsession has greatly affected the way he handles school."

Dr. Frakleman's hidden microphone caught

Frank saying to a teacher: "So, that will be four tests by Thursday, six projects by Tuesday, with a lab on the side.... And a take-home test to go. Will there be anything else with that, Mr. Warren?"

Fast-food uniforms cause substantial weight gain. After five weeks of employment at Burgers-in-a-Bag, Ernie put on forty-five pounds. "I'm sure it's the uniforms," Ernie told Dr. Frakleman. "I mean what else could it be? ... Uh, would you like to have a few of my fries? Bite of my Big-Bag Triple Burger Special? A piece of my Deluxe Cherry Pie? Sip of my Double Chocolate Shake?"

Did you hear about the woman who spent *a lot of time* at the tanning salon? Her boyfriend claimed she smelled kind of funny, a little like burnt steak. She admitted she did feel somewhat ill, so she made an appointment with the family doctor. Upon examination, the physician proclaimed, "The diagnosis is simple. You've cooked your insides...."

But wait. Don't cancel your membership at the local tanning spas just yet. Jan Harold Brunvand, Ph.D. from the University of Utah, says that this hot news flash is simply another one of those "urban myths." Dr. Brunvand told *Campus Life* magazine: "It's the kind of story that comes to you from a friend who heard it from a friend who heard it from a friend who..." Get the idea?

Of course, the toasted tanner isn't the only "urban myth" being cooked up these days. Other stories, says Dr. Brunvand, include the guy who bought a new Mercedes for $75, the couple whose pet Mexican hairless turned out to be a sewer rat, a microwaved cat, the woman whose sunlamp fused her contacts to her eyelids, and (a favorite of ours) the man who was impaled when an awkward porcupine tumbled out of a tree.

A couple of brothers have set their hopes high for earning college tuition money. Under the auspices of Afterlife, Inc., the two are selling heavenly estates to wishful thinkers. A mere $15 gets you a celestial mobile home; $100, a French chateau; $200, a condo with a pool. And, yes, many soon-to-be deadbeats are buying into the entrepreneurial undertaking. All of which proves this twist on the old P. T. Barnum saying: "There's a sucker biting the dust every minute."

GONE BANANAS

WELCOME TO WADS-O-STEREOS

The ad for a store selling stereos said you could purchase a stereo for "299 bananas." So guess what happened? Yes, thirty-two people showed up at Southcenter, a Seattle-based sound equipment company, to exchange bananas for stereos. Store officials said they had no idea that folks would not understand that "bananas" is slang for money.

But they were good sports about their gaffe: Each stereo was exchanged for $40 to $60 worth of bananas—giving the store a grand total of 11,000 bananas.

Out of the New Age ozone, we bring you yet another tale of cosmic occurrence. And this time the psychic vibes reverberated from Ann Leatherbury's golden retriever, Wham.

According to the *Wall Street Journal* (no, not the *National Enquirer*), the California (*where else*?) homemaker wanted to shed some cosmic light on her mutt's true feelings. So she hired pet psychic Beatrice Lydecker to have a little chat with Wham. Through a close encounter of the telepathic kind, Lydecker discovered that the canine desired to forgo motherhood for a "meaningful career." (*Hey, no kidding.*) Psychic Lydecker explained the yuppie puppy's innermost yearning (*and whinings*) this way: "She wants to be a show dog. She doesn't really want puppies.... [Wham] says, 'I've seen other dogs with puppies and I don't want that. It's too confining and restricting. I want to learn more, and I want to do more obedience training.'"

Charging around $50 an hour for their services, pet psychics in California are discovering that a lot of upper-crust pups have something to bow-wow about these days. They're also talking pet owners out of some hefty cash. Makes you wonder why these West Coast animal lovers don't drop by Disneyland for a day. For a lot less money, they can talk to a lot more animals ... and appear just as *Goofy*.

(But There's a Hitch)

... And an engine, and a caboose ... Sleepwalker Michael Lamont Dixon walked out of his bedroom in Danville, Illinois, one evening and ended up in Peru, Indiana—100 miles from home. Somehow this eleven-year-old snoozer boarded a train that stops near his home. He received his rude awakening the next morning when authorities found him wandering around some tracks near the small Indiana town. Michael says he doesn't remember a thing. Apparently not, or he wouldn't have ended up in _Indiana_.

To seven former students of Maharishi Mahesh Yogi, learning to fly through transcendental meditation looked like a dream come true. But the plan took a nose dive when they discovered their guru's idea of flying consisted of "hopping with legs folded in a lotus position."

Sore about not soaring, the spaced-out seven took their swami-fied sky pilot for a flight in court for high stakes—a whopping $9 million, claiming the stress on their bodies from the "so-called practice of flying" caused them to "suffer severe and continuing pain."

NEED MORE SPACE? TRY MARS!

If you're looking for a place to live that's out of this world, then you may want to check out *Martian real estate*. Richard Griffing, who claims to own Mars, told *Campus Life* he's selling 100-square kilometer lots on the red planet—*for a paltry $19.95 each*. As founder and chief executive of the (un)real estate firm, "Mars, A Planned Community," Griffing has already either sold or given away around 20,000 lots. In the near future, the outlandish land investor hopes to begin selling his high-class land deals through neighborhood convenience stores. (No doubt, we'll find info next to the *Enquirer* rack.)

With his starry eyes to the future, Griffing has even developed a few simple rules that will help when he colonizes the planet. Among them:

(1) No mobile homes.

(2) Curb your dog. "I hate it when people don't do that," says Griffing.

(3) If the claim is ever proven invalid, then no money back.

(4) Telephone solicitation will be a capital offense.

Even with his obvious enthusiasm, Griffing still wants potential investors to know both the pluses and the minuses of Martian living. "The gravitational pull is 38 percent of that on earth. And that's great for your golf game." On the negative side, Griffing admits that temeratures can drop to around 100 degrees below zero. "Hey," he adds, "I'm not going to say it'll be easy—bring a sweater."

If you do happen to be shopping around for the best buys in the solar system, Griffing offers this piece of advise: "Stay away from Venus—it's on the wrong side of the asteroid belt."

5

IF THE SHOE FITS—GO BOWLING

& Other Exciting Activities for Today's Fun-loving Sportsman

THE INCREDIBLE SHOCKING TRUTH (REALLY) ABOUT... **BOWLING SHOES!**

My career as a cracker-jack ace reporter was in a slump. We all know why, don't we? *Lockers* (see previous chapter). That's right, I'm the guy who told *Campus Life*'s readers that a bunch of goofy legislators were going to ban lockers from high school. As it turned out, I stretched the truth (just a teensy—it *was* a joke), and suddenly even my own mother wanted me exiled to Bangor, Maine. That's right, *Bangor, Maine.*

To redeem my reputation (and maybe even win me a Pulitzer) I knew I needed a story that would rock and shock the nation. Then it came to me. *Bowling Shoes*. You know, those little-understood and always-disdained objects with the weird colors and oddball soles. I knew that if I brought everybody the *real, honest-to-goodness truth* about America's most ridiculed footwear, I would no longer be the laughing-stock of the journalistic community. I might not even have to move to Bangor. Anyway, it was worth a shot.

What follows, then, are several shocking revelations, disclosed to me by experts across the nation.

Can You Say ... Ugly?

Most bowling alley employees admit it: Bowling shoes aren't the kind of footwear an Air Jordan would want to date. "Yeah, they're ugly," confesses Margaret, who hands out shoes at Lucky Strike Bowl in Tucson.

But *why* are they so ugly? While no definitive answers were revealed, most bowling shoe experts think it helps curtail a national epidemic of *bowling shoe thefts*.

Joanne, who works for a company that sells bowling shoes (along with synthetic lanes — *synthetic lanes?*), puts it like this: "Who would want to walk out of a bowling alley with a six on the back of their shoes?" Hey, makes sense to me.

Why Do Bowling Shoes Smell Funny?

The answer is rather obvious, say bowling shoe experts: *Your feet smell funny.*

Are Bowling Shoes Safe?

Klutzy bowlers, beware! Bowling shoes, confessed the experts I consulted, do not come with steel toes! Now, I should point out that a nationally known footwear manufacturer once made bronze-coated bowling shoes. "When the bowling shoe boom (see below) was taking place," says the company's vice president of International Something-or-Other, "we made these fancy, bronze-finished shoes that a lot of pros wore. But that's the closest we've ever come to steel toes." That's *really* what he said.

Effective Junior-high Repellent

According to Janet at Skaggs' All-Star Bowl in Enis, Texas, junior-high students have an especially low tolerance for bowling shoes. "They call them clown shoes," says Skaggs' main woman at the desk. "They hate 'em."

A Bowling Shoe Cover-up?

While I can only speculate, there may indeed be a bowling shoe cover-up taking place across the country! I received my first clue when I called Bowlarama in Norfolk, Virginia. Here's a word-for-word transcription of the entire conversation:

Ace Reporter: "Would you like to talk about bowling shoes?"

A rather mysterious voice: "Not really."

While not always as dramatic, similar conversations occurred over and over. Yes, time and again, bowling shoe experts refused to answer questions about the state of bowling shoes in America. Something, indeed, is going on out there. *And it doesn't appear to be good.*

Bowling Shoes Around the World

If there *is* a bowling shoe conspiracy, it's international in scope. According to the experts, bowling shoes are found in such faraway places as Australia, New Zealand, Malaysia, Indonesia, and Mishawaka, Indiana. But don't lose heart! As the story develops, your ace

reporter will be there to snoop out the *truth*, the whole *truth* and nothing but the *truth! Hey, trust me.*

Miscellaneous Other Stuff About Bowling!!!

My hard-hitting investigation also revealed:

Bowling mechanics?!? No, I don't mean automobile mechanics who go bowling (but I imagine a lot of them do). Nor do I mean throwing mechanics down the lane to knock over pins. Geeez, what do you guys take me for—a total idiot? Anyway, what I'm talking about are mechanics who work in bowling alleys. Anyway, that's what Arnold does at Channel Lanes way up in Juneau, Alaska.... I didn't even know bowling alleys *had* engines!

Phones that sound like a Canadian goose with a bad cold. While I was talking to Margaret over at Lucky Strike Bowl, I heard this loud

HOOOOWNK! HOOOOWNK!! HOOOOWNK!!!

"We have this other phone that rings like that," Margaret explains matter-of-factly. "On Friday night we Rock and Bowl—and we have to be able to hear the phone above the music."

That's right, every weekend Lucky Strike turns down the lights and a DJ plays *really loud* rock & roll to bowl by. And who says bowling's not totally hip?

The Great Bowling Boom is over! According to a big shot over at Hyde Athletic Industries in Brookfield, Massachusetts, there *really was* a bowling boom in the '50s and '60s. No, I don't mean everybody was dropping a lot of bowling balls during those years (get it?). What I mean is that bowling was really, like, *the thing to do....* Hey, are you bored and wanting to have some fun? Go to the library and look up some books on bowling that were published during the boom years. (Actually, *most* books on bowling were published during the boom years.) Anyway, check out the goofy pictures; they're a riot!

—*Chris*

Pro wrestling, you've finally met your match—*in sheer oddness, that is*. We're talking camel wrestling here, and it's big time—*in Selcuk, Turkey, at least*. Billed the Camel Wrestling Festival, this annual goofy grapple draws 25,000 fans (and close to forty pairs of camels).

Picture this: Two camels, jaws bound to prevent biting, are brought into the ring. Owners goad them into a hump-bumping battle. A camel loses the match when its hump touches the ground or when it retreats from the ring.

Not every young camel, however, can aspire to become a wrestler. According to the official rules, a grappling camel must be a male offspring of a Bactrian (two-humper) father and a dromedary (one-humper) mother. Wrestling camels begin their career at age seven and retire at about twenty-five.

Because of such strict (*and sexist*) rules, the camel capers may soon be a mere lump in Turkish history. Laments camel owner Ali Ozer: "There have been no Bactrians in Turkey for the past fifteen years. If the government does not import a few soon, this sport will be a thing of the past."

Yet if Ali and his ilk will bend the rules a bit, and if they don't mind where the hump falls, there are quite a few potbellied pro wrestlers *(of the "human" variety)* who would fit in with their ringside Bozo show.

STICK IN THE MUD

Now here's a sport with its share of ups and downs: Underwater pogo-sticking! You read right. According to *Harper's Index*, this sport takes place in the Amazon River. And just what is the longest time anyone has bounced a pogo stick under water? Over three and a half hours! ... Gee, seems like a long time to hold your breath, doesn't it?

THE OLD CODGER BOWL

If your team always loses to its arch rival, just wait and maybe you'll come out on top someday—in, say, forty or fifty years. That's what several alumni of Colfax High were hoping for recently when their old (and we mean *old*) football team suited up and asked for a rematch against St. John's.

The final score: Colfax 6, St. John's 0. And heart attacks ... miraculously, for both teams, also 0.

COW TIPS

Know what the students at the University of Kansas are doing for kicks? They're tipping cows. According to the *Kansan*, U.K.'s student newspaper, cow-tippers tiptoe into a pasture at night, look for an upright dozing cow, and run full force into her side, toppling her off her hooves. And we have received scattered reports that the sport takes place at other schools with a pasture in the back forty.

Bovine experts, however, aren't easy pushovers when it comes to believing that a half-ton cow can actually be "tipped." Jeanne Wagner, from the National Dairy Council, told us she thinks it's an in-joke that local farmers pull on naive city kids (kind of like the old snipe hunt scam). Others, like Lennie Gamage, from the Future Farmers of America, say they've never even heard of tipping. But, adds Gamage perceptively, "If a cow is tipped, I imagine it would just wake up!"

Still, some are taking the cow punching seriously. *We mean seriously.* Injuring a domestic animal would be a class A misdemeanor, punishable by up to one year in jail, says less-than-amused District Attorney Jim Flory, in the *Kansan*. Then, of course, there's the other danger: "There could be a stampede if a cow wakes up!" adds U.K. student Angela Jacobs.

Whatever the threats, whatever the dangers, be assured: Campus pranksters will continue to milk this one for all it's worth—until they get the horns by the bull.

REMEMBER THE TOMALAMO?

OK, so it's not the best way to make tomato paste. Yet for a few hundred folks from Texas and Colorado, tomato wars is the best way to *catch up* on the long-term feud that exists between the two states. Each September a few hundred saucy citizens load up their arsenal with some 15,000 pounds of overripe tomatoes, and face off somewhere near the Continental Divide. Imagine what would happen if other states decided to get involved: a little orange aid from Georgia, some gator aid from Florida, or how about some eye-to-eye combat from Idaho? *Launch the Spudniks!*

BAAA-ED IDEA

Sheep rancher Don Lewis came out looking pretty sheepish recently with his not-so-bright idea for making a few extra bucks from frustrated deer hunters. It seems that Lewis, who leases land from a national forest reserve, decided to slap some red paint on ten of his sheep, and then charge $50 to anyone who wanted to take a sheep shot at his blushing beauties. Hunters who actually bagged one would win $200. Game authorities, however, killed the idea by refusing to issue Lewis a special permit for his hunt. And as for the sheep ... it was indeed a close shave.

PUCKERED OUT

After forty-two days of locked lips, Fernando and Karen Gonzales were named the official winners of the Great American Kiss-Off. That's right— *forty-two days*.

But don't take that lip-to-lip record *too literally*. Not wanting to encourage the kiss of death, the sponsors of Reno's first kiss-athon allowed their competitors some lip-resting leeway. According to the rules, competing lip-sinkers had to smooch *just* twelve hours a day (from 9 a.m. to 9 p.m.). The puckered couples were also allowed five-minute breathers every hour.

But by any estimation, that's still a lot of time to have your lips stuck together. As a matter of fact, after that last winning pucker, Fernando told reporters, "It still feels like I'm kissing.... It's like when you wear a hat for four or five weeks and then take it off. The hat still feels like it's on."

Uh, right, Fernando. And would you say your wife is more like a derby or a Stetson?

Anyway, we're sure you're breathlessly waiting to hear how the kissed-out couple made out— *prize-wise, that is*. Would you believe ... a few thousand bucks and a condo in Idaho? *A condo in Idaho?!?*

Hey, nothing against Idaho. But, really, forty-two days should have at least earned the master kissers a split-level in Des Moines— *don't you think*?

STICK IN THE MUD

It's not at all hard to figure out how it started: A couple of farmers may have been moseying through a cornfield one day going, "Yeahp ... yeahp," when one says to the other, real slow like: "Let's go out in the pasture and watch old Bess a while. I'll bet ya a buck she'll do it over by the anthill." And so a lucrative money-raiser for charities was born in good old rural Maine. (These people *will* do anything for fun!)

Known today as "cow-plop roulette," the game has bettors placing wages on a "playing board" covered with numbered squares. After all bets are made, a well-fed cow saunters onto the "board," and well, you can guess how the game goes from there. (They *really* do this!)

But when a not-so-charitable State Police caught wind (so to speak) of the cow-pie escapades, they decided to pull the plug (so to speak). The police claimed the goofy game violates a state law forbidding the use of animals in a game of chance.

"It probably doesn't hurt the cows any," concedes State Police Sgt. Bruce Rafnell. "But it is exploitative (*exploitative*?). They are using the animals in a manner they were not designed for." (Animals were not designed to do *that*?)

Certain things just don't go together. For instance, imagine dipping shrimp in chocolate. You get the idea, right? Now, think about cardboard floats. No, no, no, we don't mean swirling cardboard bits into fudge ripple. What we're talking about here are boats made from cardboard. *It has been done.*

For several summers, the fun-lovin' citizens of Sheboygan (that's right, *Sheboygan*), Wisconsin, have defied logic (and common sense) to prove that cardboard can in fact hold together in water—*at least for a while.*

Known as the Great Cardboard Regatta, this annual event has indeed soaked up its share of publicity—along with a good portion of the Sheboygan River. It has also floated to the top as a for-real Sheboygan success story. "During the Regatta more than 20,000 people line the banks of the river," says an obviously proud Mary Jo Ballschmider, coordinator of the event. "We have people from as far away as Green Bay show up!"

As Mary Jo geared up for the fifth annual regatta, *Campus Life* asked her to recount some Great Moments in Cardboard Boating. Here are a few highlights (make that lowlights) from our conversation:

Extremely creative entries! Cardboard racing crafts don't simply look like normal boats—*or boxes.* Take the group of local principals who created a boat shaped like a gigantic No. 2 pencil (what else?). And don't miss the *point:* It was shaped *exactly like a No. 2 pencil.* "It didn't get very far," remembers Mary Jo. "The minute the principals got into the thing, it kind of just rolled over. The next year, though, they were back with the same pencil. But this time they cut it in half and used each part to make a catamaran sailboat. It worked a lot better."

Fantastic fiascoes! "Each year we give out the 'Titanic Award' for the most specta-

cular sinking," explains Mary Jo. "Last year a local fishing company entered a boat that resembled an enormous sailfish. Well, it just started bouncing up and down. It looked like a real sailfish dipping in and out of the water—until it sank."

Unprecedented embarrassments! "The first year we had the race, a group from the local yacht club made a sailboat," says Mary Jo. "A big gust of wind came along and blew them down the river and out onto Lake Michigan. The Coast Guard had to rescue them. Boy, were they embarrassed!" *No kidding.*